the MiLo & JAZZ MYSTERIES

4

THE CASE OF THE AMAZiNG ZELdA

by Lewis B. Montgomery
illustrated by Amy Wummer

The KANE PRESS
New York

Library of Congress Cataloging-in-Publication Data

Montgomery, Lewis B.
The case of the Amazing Zelda / by Lewis B. Montgomery ;
illustrated by Amy Wummer.
p. cm. — (The Milo & Jazz mysteries ; 4)
Summary: Detectives-in-training Milo and Jazz investigate whether
their town's new pet psychic is a fraud.
ISBN 978-1-57565-296-2 (pbk.) — ISBN 978-1-57565-298-6 (library binding)
[1. Mystery and detective stories. 2. Psychics—Fiction. 3. Pets—Fiction.]
I. Wummer, Amy, ill. II. Title.
PZ7.M7682Crf 2009
[Fic]—dc22
2008050212

10/09

10 9 8 7 6 5 4 3 2 1

First published in the United States of America in 2009 by Kane Press, Inc.
Printed in Hong Kong

Book Design: Edward Miller

The Milo & Jazz Mysteries is a registered trademark of Kane Press, Inc.

www.kanepress.com

For the amazing Reagan, Gwen, and Skyler

—L.B.M.

CHAPTER ONE

Milo squeezed the rubber lizard. *Squeak!* Its tongue shot out. He let go, and the lizard's tongue rolled up again.

Squeak! Roll. *Squeak!* Roll. *Squeak—*

"Milo!"

His friend Jazz stood watching him.

Quickly, he jammed the lizard on the nearest shelf. "Uh . . . I was just . . ."

"What do you think of this?" Jazz held up a yellow ball. "It comes in purple, too.

Maybe Bitsy would like purple better?"

Bitsy was Jazz's pet potbellied pig. When Bitsy got her name, she was an itsy-bitsy piglet who kept finding ways to get in great big trouble.

Now she was bigger, but still causing trouble. Yesterday she'd snitched a tuna sandwich from the table, knocked over a potted plant, and tried to gobble up a tube of lip gloss. That was why Jazz had asked Milo to go with her to Perki Pets.

"That pig has all the luck," Milo said. "When *I* do something bad, my mom doesn't buy me a toy."

Jazz laughed. "Well, the vet said we should keep her busy. Pigs only get into trouble when they're bored."

Milo sighed. He knew how Bitsy felt.

Summer vacation had just started, and already he was struggling to think of stuff to do. If only they had a new case!

Milo and Jazz were detectives in training. With a little help by mail from world-famous private eye Dash Marlowe, they solved real-life mysteries.

Jazz decided on the purple ball, and they went up to pay for it.

At the counter, a lady was telling Mr. Perki all about her cat troubles while the other customers tapped their feet and checked their watches. Milo and Jazz got in line behind a tall girl holding an exercise wheel.

"Hi, guys!" said a voice behind them. It was Spencer, a boy from their class. Milo stared at the big, brightly colored parrot perched on Spencer's wrist.

"Wow! Is that yours?" Milo asked.

Spencer's face broke into a wide grin. "My dad said if I got a good report card, I could have a pet. So I picked Floyd."

Floyd stared at Milo out of one round

eye. Then, suddenly, the parrot let out a
loud *screeeech*. Milo jumped.

"Does your parrot talk?" Jazz asked.

Spencer's grin faded. "Not exactly."

"You mean, only a word or two?"

"No," he admitted. "Nothing. I've tried
everything: 'Hello.' 'Goodbye.' 'Floyd
want a cracker?' Not a peep."

"Once I met a parrot just like that," Mr. Perki said as he rang up the exercise wheel for the girl ahead of them. "I said, 'Want a cracker?' Didn't answer. So I said a little louder, 'Want a cracker?' Still no answer."

"What did you do?" Milo asked.

"I gave up." Mr. Perki spread his arms. "I turned away. And then the parrot said—" His voice squawked. *"'Are you crazy? Birds can't talk!'"*

The kids laughed.

"Maybe it's okay that Floyd won't

10

talk," Milo told Spencer. "At least he doesn't call you crazy."

Spencer shook his head. "I don't care. I want a talking parrot."

Jazz paid Mr. Perki for the ball and took her change. "What does your vet say?" she asked Spencer.

"She just says to keep on trying."

"I guess that's all you can do, huh?" Milo said as they headed for the door.

"That's what I thought," Spencer said. "But now I've got a better plan."

"Really? What?" asked Milo.

Spencer stopped short. "I'm taking Floyd to see the Amazing Zelda."

CHAPTER TWO

"The Amazing Zelda?" Milo asked.

Spencer pointed to a sign by the door:
THE AMAZING ZELDA—PET PSYCHIC.

Jazz lifted an eyebrow. "*Pet* psychic?"

"Yeah! Lucky I saw that, huh?"
Spencer said. "Now I can find out why
Floyd won't learn to talk."

Milo reached out to touch Floyd's
bright feathers.

"Ow! He pecked me!" Milo stuck his
finger in his mouth.

Spencer smoothed the parrot's wings. "You must have scared him."

Floyd opened his beak and bobbed his head. He looked as if he were laughing.

"It's almost noon now," Spencer said. "Want to come with me?"

Jazz said, "You don't really believe this Zelda can tell you what Floyd is thinking, do you?"

"Why not?"

"Well . . . I mean . . . he's a bird."

Spencer looked puzzled. "So, you think it would be easier to read a dog's mind? Or a gerbil's?"

"Forget it." Jazz smiled. "Actually, I'm kind of curious. Let's go see this Amazing Zelda."

Milo's finger hurt. He wasn't sure he

wanted to know what Floyd was thinking.

But reading pets' minds did sound cool. Maybe he could learn to do it, too. That could be a big help on a case. Like, say a burglar broke into a house when nobody was home—except the cat. . . .

When they reached the park, a handful of kids with pets were waiting at the fountain. Most had cats and dogs. One boy held a goldfish bowl.

"Where's Zelda?" Milo asked.

"Maybe she'll pop up in a puff of smoke," Jazz said.

Spencer pointed. "Look! It's her!"

An older girl walked toward the fountain. She wore a long, flowing robe and had a red scarf wound around her head.

15

As she came closer, Milo saw that she had big, dark, spooky eyes.

The girl stood by the edge of the fountain and arranged her robe around her. Then, in a low voice, she spoke.

"I am the Amazing Zelda."

A hush fell.

Finally, a boy with a kitten piped up, "Can you really talk to animals?"

"I read their minds. I sense their needs, their wants, their hopes and fears," Zelda said. "It may come to me as a feeling, or a picture of something they've seen. . . ."

Jazz whispered, "I hope Floyd hasn't seen Spencer in his underwear!"

Zelda looked around at the pet owners. "Who will be first to test my powers?"

Everyone eyed each other nervously. Nobody answered. Then a younger girl stepped up. She held a mouse in her open palm.

"This is Coco," the girl said.

Zelda gazed at the mouse. "I sense you are having a problem with Coco."

The girl looked impressed. "That's true! I can't get her to come when I call."

She placed the mouse on the ground, then stepped back.

"Coco!" she called. "Coco!"

The mouse sat where she had put it, busily licking its brown fur.

"See?" the girl said.

Zelda picked up the mouse. Gently, she touched its head. The mouse looked up at her with bright, beady eyes.

"Mmm. Mm-hmm." Zelda nodded.

"What is it?" the girl asked.

"It's simple," Zelda said. "She won't come when you call 'Coco,' because she doesn't like that name."

"She doesn't?"

Zelda shook her head.

Jazz elbowed Milo. "Give me a break!" she whispered.

The girl looked at Zelda, baffled. "Well, then, what am I supposed to call her?"

"She says she likes . . . Annabelle."

"*Annabelle?*"

Zelda set the mouse back down. "See for yourself."

"I guess it's worth a try," the girl said. Squatting, she called softly, "Annabelle! Come, Annabelle!"

The mouse's nose lifted. Its whiskers twitched.

Then it ran straight to the girl's open hand and scampered up her arm.

CHAPTER THREE

Wow! Milo thought. Zelda was right!

All the kids around Zelda went *Ooh* and *Ahh*.

Spencer said, "Did you see that, Floyd?"

Zelda took a dollar from the smiling girl and tucked it in her robe. "Who's next?"

The boy with the goldfish stepped up. Shyly, he said, "This is Spot."

Placing her hand on the goldfish bowl, Zelda closed her eyes. Milo realized they were lined with dark makeup.

"I sense a bad feeling," she intoned. "Spot is feeling . . . jealous."

"Jealous?" the boy asked. "Why?"

Zelda's eyes snapped open. "Maybe someone else is getting more attention. Another . . . pet?"

The boy shook his head.

Quickly Zelda added, "Or something *like* a pet. Maybe a little kid?"

"My baby sister!"

The growing crowd murmured.

The boy wrapped his arms around the fishbowl. "Don't worry, Spot. You're still *my* favorite."

Now the other kids pushed forward.

"Zelda, how come my dog—"

"Zelda, I want to know—"

"Zelda, my kitty—"

The Amazing Zelda flung up a hand.

"SILENCE!"

Pressing her fingers to her forehead, she said, "One of the pets here wants to communicate with me. A pet named . . ." She looked at the parrot perched on Spencer's wrist. "Floyd."

Milo's jaw dropped. Holy cow. How did she do it?

Spencer looked excited. "You know his name!"

The other kids *ooh*ed and *ahh*ed again.

"The Amazing Zelda senses all," Zelda replied.

Spencer said, "Can you ask him—"

Zelda raised her hand. "Floyd has already told me. You are here because you want to know why he won't talk."

Wide-eyed, Spencer nodded.

Zelda tilted her head as if listening.

Floyd cocked his head back at her.

Finally Zelda said, "He's bored."

"Bored?" Spencer said. "But he has lots of toys. And we keep his cage in the living room, so he won't feel left out."

"Well . . ." Zelda paused. "He says that's good, but you're not always there."

"Yeah, but then I put on his favorite movie, *The Pirate's Parrot*. It's the one with—"

"Always the same movie?"

Spencer nodded.

"Maybe that's why he's bored," Zelda said. "He must be tired of the same old thing."

"But Floyd loves *The Pirate's Parrot*. If I turn on something else, he squawks."

"Let me try again." Frowning, Zelda laid her hand on Floyd's head. She took a deep breath. "Ahh . . . it's growing clearer."

Spencer leaned forward. "What? What is he telling you?"

"Floyd does love that movie," Zelda said. "In fact, he loves it so much that he wants to be a pirate's parrot too."

Spencer stared at her. "But . . . but he's *my* parrot!"

Zelda shrugged. "Then maybe you should be a pirate." With that, she turned away. "Next?"

Spencer held up Floyd so they were eye-to-eye. "A pirate? Are you sure?"

The parrot's head bobbed.

"Well, if that's what you really want . . ."

"Spencer!" Jazz said.

He gave her a dazed look. "Oh, um . . . Listen, I'll see you later, guys. I mean—" He deepened his voice. "Hoist the anchor, mateys. I'm shovin' off!"

As Milo stared after their classmate, he thought he heard Spencer ask Floyd, "How was that?"

Milo and Jazz stayed and watched Zelda read the rest of the pets' minds.

A girl asked why her cat seemed so happy lately. Zelda told her the cat used to hate it when she went out. "And lately you've been home more, haven't you?" Zelda asked.

"It's true!" The girl looked astonished.

Zelda told a boy who wanted another dog that his old dog would love a friend. The boy walked away beaming.

As Jazz and Milo left the park together, Milo said, "I can't believe that Floyd wants Spencer to become a pirate!"

Jazz rolled her eyes. "I *don't* believe it. If you ask me, that Zelda doesn't have a clue why Floyd won't talk. So she made something up."

"Why would she make something up when she can read his mind?" Milo asked.

"Maybe she can't," Jazz said. "Maybe some of that 'mind-reading' was really guessing. Like that boy who had the baby sister. First she said it was a pet."

Hmm. "But how did she figure out that

the mouse didn't like its name?" Milo asked. "And how could she tell so much about Floyd?"

Jazz shook her head. "I don't know." Then suddenly, she smiled. "But I know these two detectives who might be able to figure it out. . . ."

Milo grinned back at her. Their summer wouldn't be so boring, after all. Not with a new case to solve.

The Case of the Amazing Zelda.

CHAPTER FOUR

The next day, Milo was playing Slapjack with his little brother, Ethan, when the mail came.

"Here's a letter for you." His mom handed him an envelope with *DM* in the upper left-hand corner.

A new detective lesson from Dash Marlowe!

DASH MARLOWE
SECRETS OF A SUPER SLEUTH!

Predict and Test

As a sleuth, most of the time you watch and wait. But sometimes you need to shake the tree. Smoke out your suspect. Set a trap!

That's how I caught the notorious art forger Philippe Le Faux. I suspected he was painting fakes and pretending they were done by famous artists. But how to prove it?

I decided I would ask him for a picture I was sure he didn't have. If Philippe was innocent, he would say no. But if he was guilty, I predicted he would rush to paint a forgery and sell it to me.

Posing as an art collector, I tested my prediction. I asked Philippe to find a long-lost picture said to have been painted by the famous artist Pablo Picasso in 1974. I told him it was called *Three Birds, an Acrobat, or Possibly a Horse.*

The very next day, Philippe brought me the painting, signed and dated. "Here you are, Monsieur. I have found your painting from 1974, just as you asked."

"It's a fake!" I said.

As the police dragged him away, Philippe cried, "How did you know?"

I smiled. "Picasso died in 1973."

Of course, a prediction may be wrong. Until you test it, you can't be sure!

I learned this lesson the hard way—while hunting the safecracker Lefty Lou. I was convinced that the opera singer Lucia Sinistra was really Lefty Lou in disguise. So I leapt onstage during "her" solo and tried to tear off "her" wig.

It wasn't a wig.

Stuffing the lesson in his back pocket, Milo told his mom, "I'm going to Jazz's, okay?"

As usual, Ethan insisted on tagging along. He was head-over-heels in love with Jazz's pet pig, Bitsy.

Jazz answered the door. "I've been expecting you," she said.

"You have?" Milo asked.

Jazz nodded.

Ethan ran inside to play with Bitsy, and Jazz came out on the porch. She stared into Milo's eyes.

"You came here for a reason. . . ."

Milo's hand went to the paper in his pocket.

"You've got something to show me," Jazz said. "Am I right?"

"Well . . . yeah," said Milo. "It's our new—"

She lifted her hand. "Don't tell me! Let me *sense* it."

Milo frowned. What in the world was up with her? "You sound like Zelda," he said.

Jazz dropped her hand and grinned. "That's the idea."

Huh? "You want to be a psychic, too?" he asked.

"Of course not," Jazz said. "I'm just showing how it's done."

She explained that she had been doing some detective work—looking at websites about mind-reading.

"It's not so hard to fake," she said.

"You just have to act all mysterious and use a few simple tricks—like fishing."

"Fishing?" he asked.

"That's when you get people to tell you stuff without realizing it. Like suppose I say to you, 'There's somebody important in your life. Someone whose name starts with a *T*?'"

T. "Uncle Tony?"

"That's just who I was thinking of," Jazz said.

"How did you know I had an uncle whose name started with a *T*?" Milo asked.

"I didn't! That's the trick. Get it?"

Oh.

Jazz showed him the other tricks she'd written down in her notebook.

- Watch how people react to what you say. (If they smile or nod, you're on the right track.)

- Tell them what you think they want to hear. ("Your dog loves you the most!")

- Say things that have a good chance of being true.

"Like that girl with the cat," she said. "Remember? Zelda said that the girl had been home a lot more lately. Well, that makes sense! The school year's over, right?"

Milo gave Jazz the lesson from Dash. After she read it through, he asked, "How can we find out if Zelda is for real?"

Jazz tapped the paper. "What if we do the same thing Dash did?"

"What do you mean?" Milo asked.

"Test her. Pretend to be customers," she said. "We can take Bitsy."

Use Jazz's pig to test Zelda's powers!

"Great idea. Only . . . how will we know if she's reading Bitsy's mind or just using those tricks?" he asked.

"I won't give her any clues," Jazz said. "I won't even nod or shake my head. That way, Zelda will have to come up with everything herself."

A car pulled up next door, and Jazz's neighbor, Mrs. Budge, got out. She went around and opened up the back door.

Whoa. Milo gaped at a huge brown animal. "What is *that*? A cow?"

Jazz laughed. "Nope. Just a dog."

Just was not the word. That had to be the biggest dog he'd ever seen.

"Mrs. Budge is taking care of Tank while her nephew's away," Jazz said. "Want to meet him?"

"Not really," Milo said, still staring.

"Come on! He's a sweetie."

As Jazz pulled him over to the dog, Milo hung back. "Um . . . shouldn't he be on a leash or something?"

"Oh, it wouldn't do a bit of good," Mrs. Budge said cheerfully. "He's much stronger than I am."

Great.

Mrs. Budge went on. "Luckily he's very well trained. You just have to be sure not to—oh, look! He's smiling at you."

Tank's tongue hung out, oozing drool. It looked as long as Milo's arm.

He stammered, "G-good boy."

Jazz gasped.

Mrs. Budge shouted, "No!"

And suddenly, the sky was full of fur as Tank took off like a four-footed rocket aimed straight at Milo.

CHAPTER FIVE

Whoomph.

Milo found himself flat on his back,
pinned under a ton of hairy, smelly dog.

"Tank! Off!" Mrs. Budge called.

The dog obeyed. Before Milo could
move, though, Tank's gigantic tongue
gave him a slurp that drenched the
whole side of his head.

"Aw," Jazz said. "He's kissing you! Isn't that sweet?"

Mrs. Budge helped him up. "Oh, Milo, I'm so sorry. I was just about to warn you about Tankie's little . . . quirk."

His head swam. "Quirk?"

"My nephew taught him that when he was just a puppy. When he said *good*—" She paused, then spelled, "G-o-o-d b-o-y, Tank would leap into his arms and lick his face. It was the cutest thing."

"Cute," Milo echoed faintly.

"Of course, it won't do now that Tank is all grown up," Mrs. Budge said. "So we are careful not to say . . . those words . . . in front of him."

It was already past noon, so they said goodbye to Mrs. Budge, collected Ethan and Bitsy, and headed over to the park.

"Look!" Ethan said. "A pirate!"

It was Spencer. He wore an eye patch, a gold earring, and a black hat with a skull and crossbones on the front.

"Ahoy, ye scurvy bilge rats!" Spencer roared.

"Bilge rat yourself," Jazz protested.

Spencer flushed. "Sorry. No offense." He pointed at Floyd. "Got to keep him happy."

"Has he started talking?" Milo asked, then leapt back, startled, as the parrot let out a loud screech.

Floyd preened smugly. Milo couldn't decide which was worse—Floyd hating him or Tank loving him.

Spencer shook his head. "Not yet. I think it's working, though. He looked interested when I tried to teach him to say, 'Shiver me timbers.'"

"Are you a real pirate?" Ethan asked.

"No, of cour—" Spencer jumped as Floyd screeched again. "I mean, aye! Aye, me boy! Hoist the Jolly Roger! Walk the plank!"

Milo shook his head. He looked around the park. Word had gotten out about Zelda. Today there was a much bigger crowd of kids at the fountain.

Jazz led Bitsy forward. When Zelda noticed them, her eyebrows shot up.

"That's . . . that's a pig!" she said.

Jazz smiled. "I guess the Amazing Zelda really does know all."

Some of the kids near them giggled.

Zelda looked annoyed.

"So, can you tell me my pig's name?" Jazz asked.

Ethan called out, "Jazz, it's Bitsy!"

Milo clamped a hand over his brother's mouth, but it was too late.

"I knew that already," Zelda said. "Bitsy told me."

Jazz folded her arms. "All right, then. What else did she tell you?"

Zelda turned her dark gaze on the pig. After a moment she said, "You've had some problems with her."

She looked at Jazz.

46

Jazz didn't answer.

Slowly Zelda went on. "Sometimes Bitsy does something she shouldn't?"

Breaking loose from Milo, Ethan dashed up and tugged on the sleeve of Zelda's robe. "Bitsy's a good escaper," he told her. "When she was little, Jazz's dad called her Teeny Houdini."

Milo winced as Jazz gave him a dirty look. Was it his fault his little brother had the biggest mouth in town?

Solemnly, Zelda said to Ethan, "Yes, Bitsy was just telling me that."

Jazz snorted.

Zelda looked at her without speaking. Then, in her low, spooky voice, she said, "Bitsy says she runs away because she isn't treated well at home."

"What? That's ridiculous!" Jazz said.

Ignoring her, Zelda went on serenely. "She wants something you won't give her. And if you don't let her have it . . ."

"Well?" Jazz demanded.

"She says maybe she'll run away for good."

CHAPTER SIX

Jazz stormed out of the park, Bitsy in tow, and Milo didn't see her for the rest of the day.

Early the next morning, though, the phone rang. It was Jazz.

"Bitsy ran away last night!" she said.

"Again?" Milo asked.

"This is different. I can't find her anywhere." Jazz sounded scared.

"She's not in Mrs. Budge's yard?" Milo said. Another time the pig had gotten loose, she'd made a beeline for the neighbor's flowerbed.

"That was the first place I looked. The gate was open, but the yard was empty. And when I knocked, Mrs. Budge didn't answer." Jazz took a breath. "I searched the other yards, and all over the neighborhood. Milo . . . she's gone."

This was serious.

"Is there anywhere else she'd go?" he asked. "Maybe somewhere you've taken her before?"

Jazz sniffed. "Well, there's the vet, but we practically have to drag her into his office. . . . Maybe the park?"

"I'll help you look."

By the time Milo had gulped his cereal and shoved his feet into his sneakers, Jazz was at the door. Her eyes were red.

As they walked toward the park, they called, "Bitsy! Bitsy!" Milo scanned the shrubbery and peered between the houses, hoping to catch a glimpse of a snout or a tail.

Suddenly he realized that Jazz wasn't beside him anymore. He turned and saw her standing on the sidewalk half a block behind.

Jogging back, he asked, "What's up?"

Slowly she said, "I've been thinking."

"About what?"

"Yesterday, what Zelda said. . . ." Jazz looked down. "Maybe Bitsy ran away because I wasn't nice enough to her."

Milo shook his head. "That's crazy. When have you ever not been nice?"

Jazz hesitated. "Well . . . there *is* one thing Bitsy always wanted that I wouldn't let her have."

"What?" Milo asked.

"She wanted to sleep in my bed."

"Why couldn't she?"

"She huddles."

"Huh?"

Jazz explained, "It's what pigs do. They huddle together when they sleep."

"Is that so bad?" he asked.

"Do you know how much she weighs? When Bitsy huddles, I get shoved right off the bed." She sighed. "But if I'd known it meant that much to her . . ." Jazz's lower lip trembled. "Maybe I should have listened to Zelda."

Milo patted Jazz on the back. "Don't worry. We'll find her."

There was no sign of Bitsy at the park, but on the swings, Milo spotted a familiar figure in pirate getup.

"Ahoy, me hearties," Spencer said halfheartedly as they came up. "*Arrrrr.*"

From his perch on Spencer's shoulder, Floyd stared coldly at Milo.

"Still not talking?" Milo asked.

"Not a word," Spencer said sadly. "And I'm getting sick of all this pirate stuff."

"Have you seen my pig?" Jazz asked him. "She's disappeared."

"Avast!" Spencer shook his head. "That's terrible. Did you try Perki Pets?"

"Good idea," Milo said. "If anyone found Bitsy, they might bring her there."

Milo and Jazz headed up the street.

As they neared the pet store, the door

opened. A girl came out carrying a bag.
Milo had seen her somewhere before. . . .

"It's the Amazing Zelda!" he said.

The girl turned. Wearing ordinary
clothes, Zelda looked kind of . . . ordinary.
And her eyes were much less spooky
without makeup. But it was definitely her.

Zelda stared at them. She glanced nervously at the bag in her hand. Then, without a word, she quickly strode away.

"Did you see that?" Jazz asked.

Milo nodded, puzzled. It was almost as if Zelda had something to hide. But what?

Could she know something about Bitsy's disappearance?

Maybe Bitsy hadn't run away at all. Maybe she'd been . . . *pignapped*.

"We've got to catch Zelda!" Milo said. "I think she stole your pig!"

MISSING

HAVE YOU SEEN
THIS PIG?

CHAPTER SEVEN

"Stop!" Milo yelled.

Zelda was already half a block away.
She turned the corner without looking
back.

Milo ran after her, Jazz's footsteps
pounding behind him.

As they rounded the corner he saw
Zelda up ahead, walking fast.

Milo put on a burst of speed. Closer.
Closer.

He could almost touch her sleeve—

Zelda spun around and glared at him.
"What do you want?"

Milo bent over, too winded to speak.
Jazz ran up to them.

"Where is she?" Jazz demanded.

Zelda stared at her. "Who?"

"You know who."

Was that fear in Zelda's eyes?

"I have no idea what you're talking about," she said.

"Tell me! Where is my pig?"

Zelda's face cleared. "Oh . . ."

"You pignapped her, didn't you?" Milo accused. "You wanted it to look like Bitsy ran away, the way you said she would."

"Don't be ridiculous," Zelda said.

Milo pointed at the bag from Perki Pets. "What's in there? Pig food?"

Jazz made a grab for the bag. It fell, and something slid out.

Milo picked it up.

It was a package of wood shavings—the kind they used in the hamster cage in Ethan's kindergarten class.

Nothing to do with Bitsy.

Zelda snatched the package back.
"I *told* you I didn't have that pig!"

Jazz's shoulders slumped.

"I'm sorry," she said. "I just . . . I just
want Bitsy back."

The older girl gave Jazz a long look.
Then she said, "Go home. I sense your
pig has already returned."

With that, Zelda walked away.

Not knowing what else to do, the two
friends headed back to Jazz's house.

When they opened the door, they heard voices. Mrs. Budge was sitting in the living room with Jazz's dad. And on the floor—

"Bitsy!" Jazz cried.

She flung her arms around the pig.

"Mrs. Budge brought Bitsy over," Jazz's dad told them.

"How did you find her?" Jazz asked.

"Well, Tank found her," Mrs. Budge said. "Or *she* found *him*. You didn't hear the noise last night, either, then?"

Jazz shook her head.

"What a racket! I ran to the window, and there was Bitsy chasing Tank around the yard."

"Uh . . . you mean Tank was chasing Bitsy, right?" Milo said.

"Oh, no. Bitsy was furious with Tank, because he had her ball." Mrs. Budge pointed at the purple ball Bitsy was happily pushing around with her snout. "I couldn't get the ball away from Tank, and Bitsy wouldn't leave without it."

"What did you do?" Jazz asked.

"Well, it was the middle of the night, and I was sure the noise would wake up the whole neighborhood. So I brought both of them inside and went to bed."

"So she was at your house the whole time!" Jazz said. "I guess you didn't hear me when I knocked this morning."

Mrs. Budge shook her head. "After all that late-night ruckus, I slept in. And then I still couldn't get Tank to give up the ball. I had to run out and get Bitsy a new one before she'd let me take her home."

Jazz was ecstatic to have Bitsy back.

"I guess I was wrong about Zelda being a phony," she told Milo as she shook pig chow into a bowl. "She told me I'd find Bitsy at home—and I did!"

Milo did feel pretty silly about thinking Zelda was a pignapper. Still, something was bugging him. Why had she acted so nervous when they saw her outside Perki Pets?

Lying in bed that night, he sleepily shuffled the day's events around in his mind. It was like a puzzle where the pieces wouldn't fit together.

Zelda at the pet store . . . Tank stealing Bitsy's purple ball . . . Spencer in his pirate costume at the park . . . Mrs. Budge . . . Searching for Bitsy with Jazz . . .

The next thing Milo knew, the sun was shining through his bedroom window. His eyes flew open.

The pieces were slipping into place.

CHAPTER EIGHT

When Milo rang the bell, Jazz's sister, Vanessa, came to the door. "Good luck waking that girl up. I couldn't."

He ran upstairs and pounded on her bedroom door. "Jazz!"

All he heard was a muffled grunt.

Pushing the door open, he saw a lump on the bed. He yanked the covers off.

"OINK!"

Milo screamed.

Jazz sat up from the floor and rubbed her eyes. "Milo? What's going on?"

"I thought the pig was you."

"Gee, thanks," Jazz said.

He grinned. "I guess she really does *hog* the bed, huh?"

Bitsy shot Milo an offended glance,

then flopped back down and snuggled into Jazz's pillow.

"I got huddled onto the floor," Jazz said. "But it's okay. I don't want her to run away again."

"She didn't run away because of that. Remember? Mrs. Budge said Bitsy went after Tank because he had her ball."

"Yeah, but Zelda said—"

"Never mind what Zelda said," he told her. "I'm pretty sure Zelda is a fake."

Jazz looked wide awake now. "What? How do you know?"

"Mrs. Budge told us."

"She said Zelda is a fake?"

"No, not exactly," Milo said. "But she gave us a big clue. It just took me a while to figure it out."

He followed Jazz into the bathroom. While she splashed water on her face, Milo explained.

"Yesterday, when we ran into Zelda, she was coming out of Perki Pets. Right?"

Jazz squirted toothpaste on her brush. "Right. So?"

"So, who else was at the pet store yesterday morning?"

"Mmphwa 'ooky?"

"*Besides* Mr. Perki," Milo said.

Jazz rinsed and spat. "Who?"

"Mrs. Budge!" he said. "She went there to buy Bitsy a new ball."

"What does that have to do with Zelda?" Jazz asked.

"Think about it." Milo said. "Zelda was at the store when Mrs. Budge came in. And Mrs. Budge probably told Mr. Perki about Tank and Bitsy."

"Sure," Jazz said. "He loves that kind of story."

They stared at each other. A light was dawning in Jazz's eyes.

Milo went on. "If Zelda overheard the whole thing—then she *knew* Mrs. Budge was on her way to take Bitsy home. . . ."

"And that's when Zelda ran into us and told us where we'd find Bitsy!" Jazz slammed her toothbrush down. "That faker!" Then she frowned. "But what about the rest of Zelda's mind-reading? How'd she know so much about Floyd?"

"Remember the first time we saw Zelda in the park? Spencer had been talking to us at the pet store. It was pretty crowded in there that day—"

"I'll bet Zelda was at the store that time, too!" Jazz paused. "But what about Coco the mouse? How come she came when the girl called her Annabelle, like Zelda told her to?"

Milo shrugged. "I haven't figured that one out yet."

"We have to tell all the kids," Jazz said. "We can't let Zelda keep scamming them out of their dollars—"

"Hang on. We're only guessing so far," Milo pointed out. "If Zelda is a phony, we need proof."

"How can we find out for sure?"

"Predict and test, remember?" Milo grinned. "It worked for Dash, and it can work for us. We're going to set a trap."

CHAPTER NINE

"Get Tank down!" Jazz whispered. "Somebody will see us!"

"I'm trying," Milo complained, tugging on the dog's leash.

The problem was, the compact car really wasn't big enough to hide Tank. The three of them should have ducked behind something a little larger . . . like a jumbo jet.

Tank gave Milo a big, slobbery lick, and he felt saliva drip from his ear. "Thanks, but I already had a shower," he told Tank.

Jazz peeked out at the pet store across the street. "I hope Zelda shows up."

"Me, too." His clever idea about Tank didn't seem so clever now that he was drowning in doggie drool. If Zelda didn't appear soon—

"Here she comes!" Jazz ducked down.

Milo counted to twenty, then bobbed up. Zelda was nowhere to be seen.

"She's gone into the store!" he said.

Jazz and Milo swung into action. They crossed the street and tied Tank's leash to a tree in front of the pet store.

As they entered, Milo glanced down one of the aisles and spotted Zelda, out of costume, standing with her back to them. He nudged Jazz.

Mr. Perki greeted them with a smile. "Your neighbor was in yesterday," he said to Jazz. "She told me all about the pig that chases dogs."

Milo grinned. So, his guess was right!

Of course, that didn't prove that Zelda heard what Mrs. Budge told Mr. Perki. But Milo knew she could hear what they were saying now.

"That's the dog that Bitsy chased, right there." Jazz pointed. Outside the window, Tank leaned against the tree, which swayed alarmingly.

Mr. Perki whistled. "Some big dog."

"Oh, Tank's a sweetie," Jazz told him. "Kind of funny, though."

"Funny how?" asked Mr. Perki.

"Well, he knows lots of tricks. But you have to use special words. For instance, if you want him to lie down, you don't say, 'Lie down.'"

"No?"

Milo sneaked a glance at the back of Zelda's head. It was very still.

"Nope," Jazz said. "You have to say, 'Good boy.'"

Before they left, they bought a giant rawhide bone, which Tank practically swallowed whole.

As they walked him over to the park, Milo shot Jazz a grin. "So far, so good."

"That was the easy part," she said.

A crowd of kids clustered around the fountain, waiting for Zelda to arrive. The girl with the pet mouse was there again. The boy who owned Spot, the jealous fish, had shown up too.

Spencer gloomily waved a plastic pirate sword at them. Floyd leaned forward and eyed Milo's fingers.

Milo put his hands behind his back. "Hi, Floyd."

The parrot screeched.

Spencer stared at Tank. "Didn't you say you were looking for a *pig*?"

"We found her," Jazz said. "This is— well, it's a long story."

Zelda swept up to the fountain. She had put on her costume and eye makeup. The crowd pressed forward.

Holding Tank's leash, Jazz squeezed to the front. Milo was close behind. When Zelda saw them, her eyes widened.

"Zelda, you were right about my pig," Jazz announced in a loud voice. "When I got home, she was already there. I guess you really can read minds!"

Before Zelda could speak, Milo jumped in. "Come on, Jazz. I told you that was just a lucky guess. Zelda's a total fake."

"She is not!"

"Is too!"

Jazz appealed to Zelda. "Show him! Do something!"

Milo laughed. "Why don't you ask her to make Tank lie down?"

"Come on. That isn't fair—"

"Why?" he said. "If she can really read his mind, she'll know the right words to say."

They both looked at Zelda.

This was it.

For a moment, Zelda didn't move. Then she smiled slowly. "Of course I know the right words to say."

She fixed Tank with a spooky stare. And in her lowest, most mysterious mind-reader voice, she said, "*Good boy*."

Everything happened in an instant. Jazz dropped the leash. Tank soared into the air. Kids shrieked and scattered.

Whoomph.

Zelda toppled backward into the fountain with a Tank-sized splash.

"*Zelda!*" The girl with the pet mouse ran forward and hauled Zelda to her feet, dripping and sputtering. Then she turned on Jazz and Milo. "You did that on purpose! You knew that dog would knock my sister down!"

Sister? Milo and Jazz stared at one another, wide-eyed.

If that girl was Zelda's sister, then the mouse who wouldn't come . . .

Jazz lit up. "So *that's* how the mouse trick worked! Its name never was Coco, was it? It was Annabelle all along."

A faint rumble started in the crowd. *Zelda . . . mouse . . . sister . . . phony . . . trick.* The rumble grew into a roar.

And Zelda, followed by her sister, hitched up her wet robe and ran.

CHAPTER TEN

Milo slid their letter to Dash Marlowe into the mailbox, then let it clang shut.

With a curious sniff, Tank poked his nose where the letter had gone in.

"It's not coming back," Jazz told the big dog. "The Case of the Amazing Zelda is closed!"

"It never crossed my mind that the mouse could be a plant," said Milo.

"Mouses are animals," Ethan told him. "Not plants."

Jazz laughed. "Not that kind of plant. Milo just means that Zelda trained her own mouse so she could pretend to read its mind."

"That was why she acted so weird when we saw her leave the pet store," Milo added. "Zelda was afraid if we saw those wood shavings, we'd realize she had a pet mouse and put it all together."

"But we didn't," Jazz said.

They walked on toward Perki Pets. Mrs. Budge had asked them to pick up another ball for Tank.

"Something he can't chew to pieces," she had said, looking at what was left of the ball he'd stolen from Bitsy.

Milo wondered what that might be. Maybe a cannon ball?

When they walked into the pet store, they saw Spencer in shorts and a T-shirt. He was buying Floyd a bag of parrot treats.

"Ahoy, matey," Milo said.

Spencer winced. "Please, no pirate talk. I *hate* pirates!"

Floyd fluffed his feathers. He opened his beak. *"Awk! I hate pirates."*

Everyone stared at Floyd.

"Your parrot talked!" Ethan said.

Spencer's mouth dropped open. "I can't believe it. Finally! Say something else, Floyd."

"I hate pirates. I hate pirates," Floyd repeated.

Spencer sighed. "*Now* you tell me."
Everyone laughed.

"Did you get your money back from Zelda yet?" Jazz asked Spencer.

"Nope. She spent it all on toys and stuff for Annabelle. Her sister told me she's got a whole mouse playground.

A maze, a tunnel, a fancy exercise wheel . . ."

Exercise wheel. Suddenly a picture popped into Milo's head: a tall girl with an exercise wheel under her arm.

So, Zelda had been right in front of him at the pet store that first day! No wonder she knew all about Spencer's problem with Floyd.

Spencer pointed to the bulletin board. "Looks like Zelda's trying to earn more money so she can pay everyone back."

They all read: THE AMAZING ZELDA PET-SITTING SERVICE. NO PET TOO BIG OR TOO SMALL!

"I saw her in the park yesterday with three dogs," Spencer said. "And a pooper scooper."

Milo grinned. He'd have to give
Zelda's name to Mrs. Budge.

Jazz bought a big pink ball, and they
all walked outside. Tank was waiting—
drooling a river. Jazz gave him the ball.

Suddenly Floyd hopped from
Spencer's wrist to Milo's shoulder.

"Look at that!" Jazz said.

"He must like you," said Spencer.

Milo looked up at the parrot. Wow. Floyd had finally warmed up to him!

From his perch, Floyd gave Tank a long, thoughtful stare.

Then, just before he hopped off Milo's shoulder, Floyd spoke in a loud, clear voice. *"Good boy!"*

SUPER SLEUTHING STRATEGIES

A few days after Milo and Jazz wrote to Dash Marlowe, a letter arrived in the mail. . . .

Greetings, Milo and Jazz,

Parrots, pirates, and pet psychics—what a mystery! Great job solving a truly tricky case. (I *predict* it won't be your last!)

I'll bet you're tired of mind-readers, but how about some mind-*builders*? Flex your mental muscles with these puzzles and mini-mysteries.

Happy Sleuthing!
—*Dash Marlowe*

Warm Up!

These tricky questions will help keep you fit enough to tackle the toughest cases. Take a deep breath and s-t-r-e-t-c-h your brain! (Answers at end of letter.)

1. A man who owned a red sports car went down a one-way street the wrong way, but didn't break the law. Why not?
2. What happens twice in a week, and once in a year, but never in a day?
3. What kind of room has no windows or doors?
4. Two detectives are sitting on opposite sides of the same desk. There is nothing in between them but the desk. Why can't they see each other?

May I Have Your Autograph?

How do you tell a fake autograph from a real one? *Observe!* Film star Sarita Starling complained to me about people forging her autograph and then selling it. But even *she* couldn't pick her own signature from the fake ones! See how you do!

Here's her real autograph. Below are four more—three fake, one real.

Sarita Starling

1. *Sarita Starling*   3. *Sarita Starling*

2. *Sarita Starling*   4. *Sarita Starling*

Answer: 1. Fake! The *t*'s crosses on the *t*'s are too short. 2. Fake! Missing loops on the *S*'s. 3. Fake! The heart and star are switched. 4. The real one! Notice it's a little different from the other real one. People don't sign exactly the same way twice!)

Spot the Hoax (Just for fun!)

To believe or not to believe? Here are some real facts—and some made-up stories that fooled lots of people. But which is which? (You can investigate online—or just take a guess!)

1. A shark attacked a helicopter.
2. A cockroach can live for a week with its head cut off.
3. Water from a cup Elvis Presley used sold for $500.
4. A treasure cave was found in the middle of Boston.
5. An octopus escaped from its tank at a big city aquarium and survived for five days on the run.

Answers: 1. Fake. 2. True. 3. True. 4. Fake. 5. True. His name was Sid and it was his third escape. So Sid was set free in the ocean!

From Robbing to Jobbing: A Logic Puzzle

Prison was pretty boring. But three robbers, Rocky, Louie, and Sal, kept busy by each taking up a new hobby. When they were released, they all got new jobs!

Read the clues and fill in the answer box where you can. Then read the clues again to fill in the rest.

1. Louie read all 21 volumes of *The History of Hair* in the prison library.
2. One robber liked acting in the prison talent show.
3. One of the guys got a job selling jewelry at the mall.
4. Rocky's new hobby was arts and crafts.
5. After prison, Sal got a job on a TV series called *Crooks No More*.
6. Rocky didn't get the mopping job at the fancy beauty salon.

Answer Box *(see answers on next page)*

	Rocky	Louie	Sal
Prison hobby			
New job			

Boris: A Mini-Mystery

Read this mystery—and try
to draw a conclusion. . . .

Ah, parrots! One of my
most unusual cases involved
an amazing gray parrot
named Boris. The bird wasn't
friendly or chatty. He wasn't
very fond of people. But Boris could play chess! He won
match after match. And then he disappeared. *Stolen!*

My investigation led me to Mr. X, an expert chess
player who also owned a fancy pet store. One night I
sneaked into the store, ready to rescue Boris. I flicked
on a light switch—and what I saw stunned me. There,
sitting at a chessboard playing a game, was not one
gray parrot—but *two* of them!

I looked at the two birds. "Boris?" I asked.

With a chirp and a flash of feathers, one of the
birds flew straight to my shoulder. The other didn't
even look up.

The mystery was solved! I knew which parrot was
Boris. How did I know?

Answer: Boris didn't care about people, only chess. So I knew he couldn't be
the parrot that chirped and perched on my shoulder the minute he saw me.
Boris had to be the one that didn't even glance my way. (Yes—he was about to
win the game!)

Answers to the logic puzzle: Rocky got the job selling jewelry. (But in the end,
the temptation was too much. He stole some rubies and ended up back behind
bars.) After starring in the prison talent show, Sal cleaned up his act and got
a part on a popular TV series. Louie became an expert on hair, thanks to the
prison library. He got a mopping job at a fancy beauty salon and eventually
became their hair top stylist! He calls himself Monsieur Louie.

Foot Fun: Predict & Test

Detectives-in-training need lots of practice observing, making predictions, and then testing them out. Give this a try.

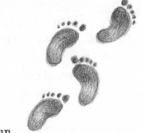

Predict! Take a good look at your feet. Read this list, and predict which statement or statements are right.

The length of your foot is the same as:
1) the distance from your wrist to your elbow
2) the length of your five toes added up
3) 15% of your total height
4) half the distance from your nose to your belly button

And now—**Test!** Take your measurements. Were your predictions right? Check below for some fun foot facts!

Foot facts: Most people's feet actually are: 1) the same length as the distance from their wrist to their elbow AND 3) 15% of their total height! (Knowing this helped me narrow down my list of suspects in The Case of the Filthy Footprints!) If your foot measures the same as statements 2 and 4, well, you're just special! Other fun foot facts: The world record for the biggest shoe size is 29.5. Each of your feet has over 250,000 sweat glands. (Hope you change your socks a lot!)

Answers for Brain Stretchers:
1. He was walking.
2. The letter *e*.
3. A mushroom.
4. They have their backs to each other.

94

Look for Milo & Jazz's first two mysteries:

★**The Case of the Stinky Socks**

Booklist, starred review

and **The Case of the Poisoned Pig**

And don't miss this spooky mystery:

The Case of the *Haunted* Haunted House

A ghost? At school? Detective duo Milo and Jazz
have their hands full when they find out their class's
"haunted house" might really be haunted!

COMING SOON

More mysteries from your favorite detectives (in training)!

ABOUT THE AUTHOR

Lewis B. Montgomery is the pen name of a writer whose favorite authors include CSL, EBW, and LMM. Those initials are a clue—but there's another clue, too. Can you figure out their names?

Besides writing the Milo & Jazz mysteries, LBM enjoys eating spicy Thai noodles and blueberry ice cream, riding a bike, and reading. Not all at the same time, of course. At least, not anymore. But that's another story. . . .

ABOUT THE ILLUSTRATOR

Amy Wummer has illustrated more than 50 children's books. She uses pencils, watercolors, and ink—but not the invisible kind.

Amy and her husband, who is also an artist, live in Pennsylvania . . . in a mysterious old house which has a secret hidden room in the basement!